The Young Performing Horse

Quentin Blake & John Yeoman

ANDERSEN PRESS

This paperback edition first published in 2016 by Andersen Press Ltd.,
20 Vauxhall Bridge Road, London SW1V 2SA.
First published in Great Britain in 1977 by Hamish Hamilton Ltd.
Text copyright © John Yeoman, 1977. Illustrations copyright © Quentin Blake, 1977.
The rights of John Yeoman and Quentin Blake to be identified as the author and illustrator
of this work have been asserted by them in accordance with the Copyright, Designs and Patents Act, 1988.
All rights reserved. Printed and bound in China.

1   3   5   7   9   10   8   6   4   2

British Library Cataloguing in Publication Data available.

ISBN 978 1 78344 375 8

Vicky and Bertie were twins. Every day when they came home from the village school they used to help their mother and father with all the jobs on the farm.

One evening Farmer Priddy said to his wife: "Vicky and Bertie have a long journey to and from school every day. I think they deserve a little horse of their own." Mrs. Priddy agreed.

Saturday came and Vicky and Bertie got up early to walk to the market. Their parents saw them off at the farmhouse gate.

"Come back as soon as you can," said Mrs. Priddy.

"You can't spend more than two guineas, remember," said their father, handing Bertie the two gold coins tied up in a knotted handkerchief.

When the twins arrived at the market the horse auction had already started. They had to push their way through a crowd of cheery red-faced farmers, all dressed in hairy tweeds and smelling of beer and tobacco.

At last there was only one strange little creature left. It made a kind of bow to Vicky and Bertie.

"This one is, er… a real rarity," said the auctioneer. "It's… er… a Young Performing Horse."

The horse was certainly unusual, with his big eyes, long eyelashes, baggy skin, thick legs and shiny black hooves. The twins fell in love with him immediately.

"I'll give you two guineas for him," shouted Bertie.

"He's yours," said the man.

On the way back to the farm they stopped to unpack their sandwiches. "I'll collect some hay for our Young Performing Horse," said Bertie. But when he offered the little horse the hay, it just shook its head and blinked its eyes longingly at their sandwiches.

So they gave him some sandwiches. And when Vicky and
Bertie sat down on the grass to eat, the back end of the Young
Performing Horse sat down too. "He's a real rarity," said Vicky.
"I've never seen a horse like it in all my days," said Farmer Priddy.
"Mind you, it's too small to carry you to school yet," said
Mrs. Priddy.

However, the next Monday, when the twins set out for school, the Young Performing Horse trotted along with them. It was a small school, with only one teacher – Miss Sampler. She let Vicky and Bertie sit with their Performing Horse at the back of the class. The Young Performing Horse went to school every day, and not only did he behave himself beautifully in class but he even learned his lessons. He did his sums, and gave the answers by tapping his hoof on the desk.

He could point to any country on the globe.

He could spell simple words by picking out the letters on cards.

And he kept time perfectly in the folk-dancing practice.

Hard times came. The crops failed and Mr. Priddy had to sell many of his animals.

"Don't sell the Young Performing Horse," begged Vicky and Bertie. "He'd only fetch two guineas, and we're sure that we could make our fortune with him if you'd let us go to London." Mr. and Mrs. Priddy at last gave in. Miss Sampler gave the twins the address of her old friend Mr. Crumbles who owned a theatre in London and might give them work.

There were tears in Mrs. Priddy's eyes as she wrapped a woollen scarf around each of the three necks.

"Don't cry, Mother," said Bertie as they set out. "We'll write a letter every day, and come back as soon as we've made our fortune."

Vicky, Bertie and the Young Performing Horse trudged through the snow until they reached the big city.

They had never seen so many people before. It was growing dark by the time they found Mr. Crumbles' theatre.

Outside was a large notice with the words:
VINCENT CRUMBLES' JUVENILE THEATRE.
YOUNG ACTORS REQUIRED.
"That's us," said Vicky. "We'll make our fortunes as actors."

And the three of them went through the stage door and on to the stage, where they found Mr. Crumbles. He was surrounded by lots of noisy children dressed as pirates, fairies, footmen and devils.

Mr. Crumbles was pleased to see Vicky and Bertie; but he wasn't very cheerful. "Business is bad," he said. "A rival company — Signora Provini and her Performing Dogs — has just opened across the road, and no one wants to see our plays any more."

"They will if you let our Young Performing Horse have a part," said Vicky and Bertie, and they made him show Mr. Crumbles what he could do.

"He's a dramatic genius! A real rarity!" said Mr. Crumbles. "I'll write him a leading part in 'Aladdin' and design a new poster immediately."

That night the theatre was full of people who had seen the new posters. The Young Performing Horse had the whole audience in fits of laughter as he covered the stage with wallpaper and paste in the decorating scene. He was having the time of his life.

Mr. Crumbles was amazed. "It was the most successful
performance we have ever given. That Young Performing Horse
will be world-famous one day, believe me."

Soon all London had heard about the Young Performing Horse. Crowds collected outside Mr. Crumbles' theatre to see him.

The audiences roared with laughter when he made such a mess of the kitchen in the cookery scene in 'Cinderella'.

And when he made fun of the teacher in the school scene in 'Babes in the Wood'.

And when he pretended to get frightened in the haunted house in 'Jack and the Beanstalk'.

In fact, the Young Performing Horse became so famous that one day Mr. Crumbles received a letter summoning the whole company to give a Royal Command Performance at Buckingham Palace.

They were all introduced to the Queen. The boys had to bow and the girls had to curtsey. The Queen was most impressed when the Young Performing Horse did a bit of both.

"We are ready for the performance to begin," said the Queen.

"And stop pulling his tail, Teddy," she added, turning to her son, a fat boy in a kilt.

The Young Performing Horse's antics with Vicky and Bertie in the woodland ballet scene from 'Red Riding Hood' were so funny that even the Queen was highly amused.

At the end of the performance the Queen congratulated them all. "Wonderful!" she said. "If only all my people could see a Young Performing Horse this Christmas."

'What a marvellous thought," said Mr. Crumbles. "But that's impossible: there is only one Young Performing Horse."

"I've got an idea," said Bertie to Mr. Crumbles.

Back at the theatre, Bertie explained his idea to the company.
Soon they were all busy with the legs of old corduroy trousers,
scraps of felt, pieces of string and paint – stitching together
costumes that looked remarkably like the Young Performing Horse.

Two children got into each costume. During the weeks that
followed the Young Performing Horse taught them all how to
trot and dance and do all the comical things that he had done
on stage.

At last the imitation horses could all step in a bucket of paint as well as their teacher himself.

That Christmas children did their imitation of the Young
Performing Horse in theatres all over the country. The audiences
were absolutely thrilled. The idea made Mr. Crumbles and
his company so rich that Vicky and Bertie were able to buy
new animals for the farm. And Mr. and Mrs. Priddy, and Miss
Sampler, were delighted to come to London to see Mr. Crumbles'
latest show – starring Vicky, Bertie and the original Young
Performing Horse.